GATORS & TATERS
A WEEK OF BEDTIME STORIES

BY ELAINE AMBROSE

ILLUSTRATIONS BY PATRICK BOCHNAK

Mill Park Publishing

GATORS & TATERS

A WEEK OF BEDTIME STORIES

BY ELAINE AMBROSE

ILLUSTRATIONS BY PATRICK BOCHNAK

Mill Park Publishing

Text Copyright © 2017 by Elaine Ambrose
Illustrations Copyright © 2017 by Patrick Bochnak

For information regarding permission, write to:
Mill Park Publishing
PO Box 1931
Eagle, ID 83616
Email: elaine@millparkpublishing.com

Library of Congress Cataloging-in-Publication Data
Ambrose, Elaine
Gators and Taters: A Week of Bedtime Stories

Summary: Original stories to be read to children.

Library of Congress Number (First Edition): 2003101287

ISBN: 978-0-9975871-0-4

Also available in eBook and Audiobook versions

Printed in the U.S.A.

First Edition, 2003
Second Edition, 2017

FOR MY CHILDREN, EMILY AND ADAM

YOUR SPIRIT IS MY JOY.

I enjoyed telling stories to my children when they were young, and now I continue the tradition by sharing tall tales with my grandchildren. Inspiration for this children's book originated while cross-country skiing in the mountains of central Idaho. A subsequent journey to Ireland rekindled my interest in folklore and storytelling.

– Elaine Ambrose

CONTENTS

GATORS & TATERS

Old Wendell O'Doodle, a hard-working man,
enjoyed his job daily of driving a van.
He traveled the roads and he went everywhere
transporting his cargo from here over there.

Now Wendell O'Doodle was hired one day
to do a hard job that was far, far away.
He had to be brave, that mattered the most,
to take a large crate to the Oregon Coast.

Well, inside the box and along for the ride
were two alligators named Cleo and Clyde.
Across the whole country their journey began
in Wendell O'Doodle's bright traveling van.

They crossed the wide prairie and all they could see
was more prairie coming as flat as could be.
And then came a canyon so deep and so wide
that Cleo and Clyde stayed curled up inside.

The mountains were awesome with green trees and snow
and Wendell was careful, and slow he did go.
Then five days went by on their long journey west
and Idaho came so they took a good rest.

He parked his big van by a field full of green,
with the biggest potatoes that Wendell had seen.
His passengers suddenly went on alert
as Wendell got down and he dug in the dirt.

He pulled up a bush at the end of the row
and found some potatoes all ready to go.
"I love new potatoes," he said with delight.
"I must find the farmer and buy some tonight."

He went to the crate full of Cleo and Clyde
and told them politely to stay safe inside.
He gave them some water and blueberry pie,
then walked down the road as he called out, "Bye-Bye."

Well Cleo and Clyde didn't like that a bit!
They became so annoyed that they worked up a fit.
"I'm tired of riding," said Clyde with a pout,
and he pushed at the lock with his long slimy snout.

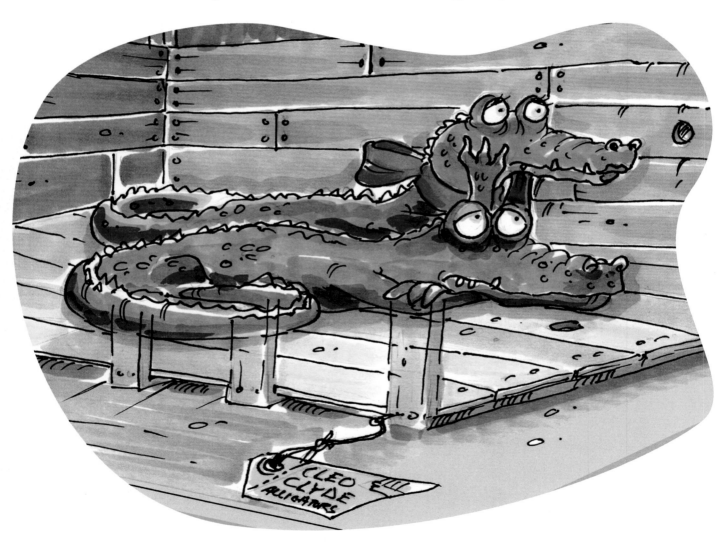

Then Cleo rolled over and punched with her tail
and the lock fell apart on their traveling jail.
"We're free! Let's go wander!" the passengers cried.
And out of the van wiggled Cleo and Clyde.

They rolled in the dirt and smashed bugs with their toes
and marched through the field between long bushy rows.
Their escape from the crate was a wonderful treat
and they laughed right out loud and clapped all of their feet.

They dug up potatoes and gobbled a bunch
while Cleo was singing, "Let's have these for lunch!"
"Potatoes are tasty," Clyde said with a sigh.
"I like them much better than blueberry pie."

The field of potatoes was such a cool place
that Cleo and Clyde had a fun gator race.
They wiggled and giggled as fast as they could
but rambled much farther than anyone should.

The sunlight was fading when Cleo stood still,
"I think we are lost and I do feel a chill."
She looked at the dark sky and muttered to Clyde,
"I hope we get back to continue our ride."

But Clyde felt so good from his tail to his chin.
"I don't WANT to go back," he exclaimed with a grin.
"I love these potatoes, I love being free,
I love running long rows with you next to me."

"I like these green fields, and I like you the most.
Let's NOT go along to the Oregon Coast!
We have water and sunshine and plenty to eat,
so PLEASE stay with me and our life will be sweet!"

Soon Cleo discovered that farm life was grand
as she stayed and she played on the nice farmer's land.
They laughed and they sang as they wandered the rows
and juggled potatoes with toes and with nose.

Poor Wendell O'Doodle became a sad man
when he came back that night to his dark, empty van.
His cargo was gone, there was nothing inside,
and he never did find charming Cleo or Clyde.

He thought to himself as he drove the next day,
"The Oregon Coast is a fine place to stay.
I'll get me a home and then not have to drive,
and I'll grow some potatoes to keep me alive."

The farm life delighted those silly young gators.
They munched and they lunched on the acres of taters.
And often at night came the laughter outside
from those fun alligators named Cleo and Clyde.

THE BIRTHDAY BOY

When Adam was two years old in October, his mother made a birthday cake that looked like a pumpkin. The round, chocolate cake smeared with orange frosting had a grinning face made from candy corn. Adam sat in his high chair, clapped his hands and squealed with delight when his mom showed him the treat.

He didn't quite understand why people were singing to him or why his father lit two candles, but he knew there was something special about him on this day.

His mom removed the candles and candy corn and then placed the pumpkin cake in front of him. Suddenly, Adam smashed his face into the frosting! Lifting his head with chocolate crumbs and orange frosting smeared all over his cheeks, he laughed and licked his lips.

"Birt-day boy!" he yelled.

Then he smashed his face into the cake again, gobbled a bit and washed it down with milk from his plastic cup. Everyone laughed. Adam was happy.

Adam's parents, grandparents, an aunt, and young cousin came to his party. After everyone ate and cleaned up, they gave presents to Adam. He tore the paper off one and found a new ball.

"Yah!" he exclaimed.

Then he unwrapped a pair of socks. "Boo!" he yelled.

Next came a large package from his grandmother. Inside he found a big stuffed bird, like the ones he loved to watch on his grandparents' farm.

"Buster Eaglebeak!" Adam exclaimed. He was so happy he almost cried. What a wonderful day!

The next morning, Adam climbed out of his crib, grabbed Buster Eaglebeak, and ran into the kitchen. His mother was making breakfast.

"Birt-day boy!" he yelled, clapping his hands.

His mother kneeled in front of him and kissed his cheek.

"Your birthday is over, Addy Paddy," she said softly. "But you are still two years old!"

She helped him hold up two fingers. He didn't know what she was talking about.

"Cake!" he demanded. "Me birt-day boy!"

His mother smiled and picked up her confused son. "Someday you'll understand," she said. "Want some juice?"

Adam put Buster Eaglebeak on the counter, sat in his high chair and quietly sipped his juice. There were so many things he didn't understand. Why did his party have to end? Why couldn't he have cake every day? Where were more presents? What was so special about holding up two fingers?

That evening, his mother rocked him in the big wooden rocking chair in his bedroom. He was still confused about being the birthday boy, but he felt better as she sang to him:

Don't worry, my son, I want you to know
I'll love you forever, wherever you go.

* * *

Three years later, it was Adam's fifth birthday. By then, he had learned all about getting older and was prepared for a party with cake, presents, and friends having fun.

On the morning of his birthday party, he was so excited that he ran all through the house yelling, "I'm the birt-day boy!"

His younger sister, Jane, was only three years old. She didn't understand what he was doing, but she started running around and yelling, too.

"Hey, you, stop!" shouted Adam. "I'm the birt-day boy, not you!"

Jane started to cry and their mother came in to see what was happening. She kneeled and gathered Adam and Jane in her arms, then calmed them by singing,

Don't worry, my children, I want you to know
I'll love you forever, wherever you go.

Adam wasn't mad anymore. He tried to explain to Jane about birthdays. He helped her hold up three fingers and showed her his five fingers.

"It's hard to understand," he told her. "But when you're big like I am, you'll know why I'm the birt-day boy and you're not."

Five children came for the party and Adam eagerly opened his presents. There was a toy airplane, a football, a book, a bucket of clay, and a whistle. They played in the yard while his mother prepared cake and ice cream. Jane rolled in the wrapping paper and ribbons singing "Birt-day boy, birt-day boy."

That night, Adam took his presents to his room. Buster Eaglebeak, a bit worn and tattered, still sat on his bed. Adam picked up the toy and placed it with his new presents.

"Don't worry, Buster," he whispered to the toy. "I still like you, too."

* * *

Five years later, on Adam's 10th birthday, he woke up and sang out loud, "I'm the birthday boy today!"

By this time, Buster Eaglebeak had been moved to a shelf in his bedroom closet. Adam said "Good morning" to the old toy and then hurried to the kitchen.

His mother had the red "You Are Special Today" plate on the table. She fixed pancakes and wished him a happy birthday. To celebrate it, she and his dad were taking Adam and some of his friends to a video game arcade after school. Then they would have pizza and cake.

"Mom," Adam said as he got ready to leave for school. "Am I too big for a birthday party?"

His mom put her hands on his shoulders. He was so tall that she didn't have to kneel anymore. Smiling, she said, "Today you are the birthday boy and you should celebrate." Then she whispered,

"Don't worry, my son, I want you to know
I'll love you forever, wherever you go."

Adam smiled and hurried out the door.

* * *

Five years later, Adam was 15. No big party was planned, but his two best friends were taking him to a movie. That night as he started to leave, his mom called him to come into the kitchen. Because he was so tall, she had to reach up to put her hands on his shoulders.

"Hey, birthday boy," she whispered. "Have fun, but don't forget: I want you to know I'll love you forever, wherever you go."

Everyone was asleep when Adam got home after the movie and went to his room. As he hung up his athletic jacket, he saw Buster Eaglebeak under a stack of clothes.

"Silly bird," he said, grinning.

* * *

Almost four years later, Adam was cleaning out his bedroom. In just a few days he would leave for college. Finding dusty old Buster Eaglebeak, he smiled, and gently placed the toy in a box marked "Adam's Treasures. Put in storage."

Just then his mother came into the room and saw Buster perched in the box of toys.

"Remember when you were the birt-day boy?" she asked Adam. "That seems like only yesterday. And now you're off to college, and I won't even see you on your birthday."

She was amazed at how tall her son had grown over the summer. "Be sure and eat well," she said. "And don't forget to call every Sunday."

He turned and smiled at her. Then he leaned down and whispered,

"Don't worry, Mom. I want you to know
I'll love you forever, wherever I go."

HOOTENFLOOT FLIES THE COOP

Two little ladies lived at home,
content and sure to never roam.
Their tiny cottage full of charm
protected them from outside harm.

Miss Bitterpenny, thin and proud,
was known to mutter things out loud.
She always dressed in black or blue,
and drank flamdoogle tea at two.

Miss Wobblefloss was short and funny,
cheerful, bright, and sweet as honey.
Wearing hats with purple stars,
she loved to munch on chocolate bars.

Each evening they would sit in chairs
and eat three bowls of pickled pears.
They'd guzzle mugs of pumpkin juice,
with corncob cakes and buttered goose,
then to the porch to rock until
the lights went off in Puddingville.

They had a pet out in the tree,
a funny owl that sang for free.
The ladies named him Hootenfloot
and tossed him bags of tickle fruit.

He built a tree house, warm and cute,
and sang but never gave a hoot.
And so, their life was never foul,
two simple ladies with their owl.

But then one bluster blossom day
a horrid sadness came their way.
"Oh no," they cried in great despair,
"our Hootenfloot's best branch is bare."

They searched the mangled moss for clues
and trampled through the muckdrip slues.
They called beyond the limestone logs
and poked beneath the crawdad bogs.
Alas! The truth just made them droop:
good Hootenfloot had flown the coop!
Their sadness rained like tuba tears.
It soaked the ground for 20 years.

One wobbly willow day in fall,
a passing traveler came to call.
The friendly Doctor Dimpledoodle
was chewing on some sausage strudel.
Then seeing tears that would not end,
he stopped to be their only friend.
"Oh, dear," he sighed. "You are so glum.
Please share with me a bramble plum."
He picked the fruit from yonder sack
and pulled the purple peeling back.

The ladies loved the bramble plums
and licked their fingers and their thumbs.
Miss Wobblefloss began to talk,
but choked up as if eating chalk.

Miss Bitterpenny stood to speak,
then dabbed a doily at her cheek.
"Please help us, doctor, if you could.
Our tears and fears make life no good.
Sweet Hootenfloot, our happy friend,
has left a wound that cannot mend.
He disappeared without a word,
and how we worry for that bird.
We sit each night and mourn the time
and eat stale buns with mango slime."

The doctor heard their woeful tale,
while pouring spruce juice from a pail.
He gulped it down and wiped his lips,
then tied his pack around his hips.
"Now don't you fear," he told the two.
"I'll find dear Hootenfloot for you."
He donned his hat and winked his eye,

secured his pack and waved good-bye.
Miss Bitterpenny grasped her hands
and wished him well in foreign lands.
Miss Wobblefloss just wiggle-clapped
and jumped until her apron snapped.

The doctor traveled many days
and went about in many ways.
He rambled first inside a boat,
then roller-skated with a goat.
He sat in carts pulled by a toad
and slept in wagons down the road.
He sang sweet songs with silly words
while searching skies for wayward birds.

Until one day he saw a sign:
"Come Hear an Owl That Sings So Fine!"
He found the owl tied to a post
just singing songs for bits of toast.
The doctor sat beside the bird
and listened to each sorry word.

"I was so happy in my tree,
but not content to be just me.
I thought my life could be so grand
if I explored a different land.
I flew to find a place so cool
where I could live without a rule.
I painted spots upon my beak
and took a bath just once a week.
I danced beneath the foofum shrub
and ate kabongas by the tub.
But then when leaves began to fall
I didn't have a friend at all.
I cried into my tiny towel,
a sad and sorry, lonely owl!
I got a job here on this post
just singing songs for milk and toast.

Oh, doctor, see how I am ill.
I miss my life in Puddingville.
Miss Bitterpenny wanted me
to sing her songs from up the tree.
Miss Wobblefloss gave me sweet cake.
Can she forgive my bad mistake?"

The doctor gave a happy howl.
He hugged the frumpy, lumpy owl.
"Come home with me, you silly bird,
and we will have the final word.
Your place is in your tree house there
upon your perch behind the stair.
I'll pay to take you from this place
and we will wash your frowny face.
We'll get a hambone hat to wear
then buy potato cakes to share."

Thus off they went to find his home,
so Hootenfloot no more would roam.
The ladies cheered and stomped their feet
and danced and whistled in the street.
They made a sign with jelly foam,
"HEY HOOTENFLOOT, WE'RE GLAD YOU'RE HOME!"

They threw a party with balloons,
invited friends and drew cartoons.
Miss Bitterpenny dressed in red
and wore bananas on her head.
Miss Wobblefloss was happy, too.
She laughed until her nose turned blue.
They gave the doctor popcorn pies
with jars of snowballs for his prize.
So Doctor Dimpledoodle sat
and made each one a party hat.

The owl flew high atop the trees
to sing sweet songs into the breeze.
Yes, brighter days came back quite soon
with Hootenfloot's new happy tune.
All Puddingville is doing well.
And that's the end of this fine tale.

THE SECRET READING ROOM

Amber was nine years old when she first discovered the secret reading place in the attic of her grandmother's old farmhouse. The room was her reward for helping to make applesauce.

Amber and her grandmother had worked in the kitchen all morning, peeling and slicing apples. After mixing the slices in a big pot on the stove, they added water, cinnamon, sugar, and nutmeg. Then they spooned the hot mixture into quart jars, screwed on lids, and steamed the jars until the lids popped shut.

After the jars cooled, Amber and her grandmother took them to the pantry beyond the kitchen. Amber slid the applesauce onto shelves next to colorful jars of peaches, green beans, and tomatoes. Her farm family had repeated this autumn ritual for several generations.

"Thank you for your help, Amber," her grandmother said, looking at the shelves full of fruits and vegetables. "This will last us all winter."

Then the grandmother smiled at Amber. "I want to show you a place where I used to go to read," she said. "I was about your age then."

Amber's grandmother pulled on a rope connected to a door in the ceiling. Suddenly the door swung down and a ladder emerged from the hole. She pulled on the wooden ladder and it slid to the floor with a thump.

"Come on up," called Amber's grandmother as she started up the wooden ladder.

Amber hesitated, then followed her into the attic. When her grandmother turned on the light, Amber could see old trunks, dusty boxes, an antique sewing machine, and stacks of books.

"Wow!" Amber exclaimed. "This stuff must be hundreds of years old."

Her grandmother laughed. "Not quite," she said. "But it makes a great place to escape from the world."

Pointing to a door at the end of the room, she said, "There. That's your new reading room."

Amber tiptoed across the floor and tugged on the door. It opened with a creaking sound. She found the light switch and turned on the single bulb hanging from the ceiling. Her eyes opened in amazement. The room had paneled walls covered with old travel posters. Paris. Egypt. Ireland. Italy. Hawaii. India.

An old stuffed chair sat in the corner, surrounded by bookshelves bulging with travel books. A puff of dust escaped as Amber sank down into the chair. She eagerly pulled out a book and opened to a page showing a map of the world.

"Why didn't you tell me about this place?" she asked in amazement.

"I was waiting for you to be ready," her grandmother said, with a twinkle in her eye. "You can go anywhere from this room."

The grandmother smiled and turned to go back downstairs. "Stay as long as you want," she said. "I'll bring you some snacks later."

Amber loved to read, especially about people in distant lands. Daily life on the farm didn't provide many opportunities for travel, but she knew that someday she would go down the road and find adventure. Now alone in the secret reading room, Amber selected a stack of books and settled into the big chair.

The first book was on Ireland. She read about Molly, a girl from Galway who danced to the energetic music of flutes and accordions. Molly wore colorful, starched dresses covered with traditional designs. With her arms straight down at her sides, she covered the dance floor in rhythm to the music, stomping on her heels, kicking her legs, and twirling on her toes.

Molly lived with her family in a small white house at the edge of Galway Bay. Her father was a fisherman and her mother sewed lace curtains for sale in the village. Molly and her sisters and brothers worked in the garden and tended a flock of sheep. They rode bicycles to school and all of them played musical instruments. From the picture in the book, Molly seemed to smile at Amber and invite her to Ireland.

"Someday," whispered Amber, "I'll go there."

Amber picked up another book, this one on India. She read about a girl named Agra who dressed in long silk gowns and wore jade necklaces, gold bracelets, and rings on her fingers and toes. She was tall, with dark eyes and long black hair. Agra worked with her family creating marble tables of all sizes. She helped select and polish the precious stones they would combine in colorful designs and set into the tabletops. The craft had been in her family for hundreds of years.

Every morning, Agra went to the community well to get water to bring back to their small, tidy shop. She carried her jug through busy streets full of people, cattle, merchants, bicycles, and pushcarts of produce. Incense filled the air, along with the sounds of flutes and tingling bells. Travelers munched on pita bread filled with curried chicken. A frustrated man tried to get his camel to walk faster. Men in white tunics sat in doorsteps puffing on long pipes.

Agra seemed to call to Amber to join her in the morning walk. Amber stopped reading and imagined how life would be on the other side of the world.

The next book was about Hong Kong. Amber read of Lucy, a girl who lived with her parents in a tiny apartment in the city. Lucy was small with black hair and white skin. She wore a uniform to school and could speak four languages. Her favorite meal was shrimp with fried seaweed and sweetened red bean cream.

When her parents were not working, they would take Lucy to the open markets throughout the city. She loved to see the selection of frogs, snakes, turtles, and birds for sale. Her mother purchased silk or jade jewelry and her father looked through selections of scrolls – ancient writings on rolls of paper. In the evening, they would walk out on the pier and watch the boats coming and going in the harbor. As with most children in Hong Kong, Lucy was the only child in her family. Amber imagined she needed a friend.

Amber was getting sleepy, but had time for one more book. She selected one about Hawaii. She read about Mele, a young Hawaiian girl who lived on the island of Maui. She wore colorful dresses, and she made necklaces from fresh flowers. Mele usually went barefoot unless she was at school. She loved to play on the beach with her friends and swim in the warm ocean.

Mele and her sisters worked with their mother in a café in Paia. They made fish cakes, green salads, and coconut macaroon cookies. If the café closed early for the day, their mother would take them up-country for a picnic in the mountains. From the hillside, they could see both sides of the island and watch the huge tourist ships sail into view. As Amber read, she wondered what it would be like to live on an island.

"Amber, dear," her grandmother called as she climbed the ladder. "You have been here all day. It's time to come down."

Her grandmother walked into the reading room with a plate of fresh-baked cookies. Amber took a bite of one and chewed slowly.

"Can I come here again?" she asked.

"Of course." Her grandmother smiled. "This is your special room now."

Amber started to follow her grandmother, then she turned and looked back into the travel room. She thought she saw Molly, Agra, Lucy, and Mele smiling from the posters on the walls. But it

was just her imagination. She turned off the light and went down the ladder.

That night in bed, Amber could hardly sleep. She tossed and turned, hearing music and dancing in Ireland, smelling smoky incense in India, tasting fried seaweed in Hong Kong, and watching the blue ocean wash white beaches in Hawaii. When she finally fell asleep, she dreamed of new adventures and new friends. She knew she would travel the world, at least from her secret reading room. There were hundreds of people and places yet to discover.

MAMA, I'VE HAD A BAD DAY!

Mama was reading a book in her chair,
enjoying the quiet with no one else there,
when all of a sudden, the door opened wide
and Andrew, the oldest, came running inside.
His face was all red and his hair was untamed.
He threw down his book bag and loudly proclaimed:
"Mama, oh Mama, I've had a bad day!
I do not like school so I'm running away!
I don't like math and I can't do the art.
I want to learn more and I know that I'm smart.
I once raised my hand but my answer was wrong.
I won't go to school 'cause I do not belong!
Mama, oh Mama, I can't keep on track.
I'd rather play baseball. Don't make me go back.
I'll be a good boy if I just stay away.
Oh Mama, oh Mama, I've had a bad day!"

He sat down beside her with such a sad look,

she went to the bookcase and pulled out a book.

The pages held photos of sweet, happy faces,

of fun times, vacations, adventures, and places.

He looked at the pictures of teammates and friends,

and thought of his games that his family attends.

His mama spoke proudly and eased all his dread,

"You're a hero to me, son," she lovingly said.

"Remember that day when your hit won the game?

Your team was excited and screamed out your name!

So, don't be so sad, son. This day has been spent.

Just think of your school as a sporting event!"

So, Andrew felt better and finished the book,

then went to the kitchen for something to cook.

They mixed up some crackers and cheese dip and juice,

and Andrew felt better and offered a truce.

"I'll go back tomorrow," he said with a grin.

"I'll work with my teacher to help our team win."

He finished his snack and then took off to play.

"Thanks, Mama," he hollered, "you saved my bad day!"

So, Mama was happy with Andrew the winner

and started to fix some spaghetti for dinner.

When out in the hall there arose such a roar
that Mama dropped pasta all over the floor.
Then into the room came first-grader Michelle,
just crying and shouting with more woe to tell.
"Mama, oh Mama, I've had a bad day!
Nobody likes me. I'm running away!"
She threw down her backpack and slumped in the chair,
her face was distorted in total despair.
She let out a wail and then wiped off a tear
then called for her mama to "Come over here!"

"The boys will not let me join them in their games,
and the girls say I'm silly and call me bad names.
They will not take turns and they never pick me,
so, I sit by myself 'til the bell rings at three!"
Her mama came over and gave her a kiss,
and took down the scrapbook and said, "Look at this!
Now here is a photo to bring you some cheer.
Remember your birthday with all the kids here?
Your friends had great fun and went to the park,
ate ice cream and cake, and then laughed until dark.
and here is a picture of you in the choir.
The others adored you 'cause you could sing higher."

They looked through the book full of friends and fun days,
remembering parties, and soccer, and plays.
They laughed at her best friend, who looked such a fright
when they dressed as space monsters on Halloween night.
She then saw a girl who had moved far away.
She said, "I sure miss her. I'll call her today!"
The book full of smiles was definite proof
that saying "They LIKE me!" was really the truth.
They counted the people who knew her quite well,
deciding that many were fond of Michelle.
The girl dried her tears that she thought would not end,
and ran to the phone to call up her best friend.
Her mama was happy to have one less stress
and went to the kitchen to clean up the mess.
Just when she was ready to finish the meal
she heard frantic sounds from the baby's loud squeal.
Into the room came sweet Jamie, just three,
who was crying, and sighing, and mad as could be.
"Mama, oh Mama, I've had a bad day.
My brother and sister – they won't let me play!
That Andrew is working on papers for you.
He won't let me help with my crayons and glue.
Michelle and her friends have a playhouse outside.

They told me to leave it and run off and hide.
They say I'm too little, to go find my mother.
But I want to play with my sister and brother!"
She jumped on the couch with a teary-eyed look,
so, Mama again got the big photo book.

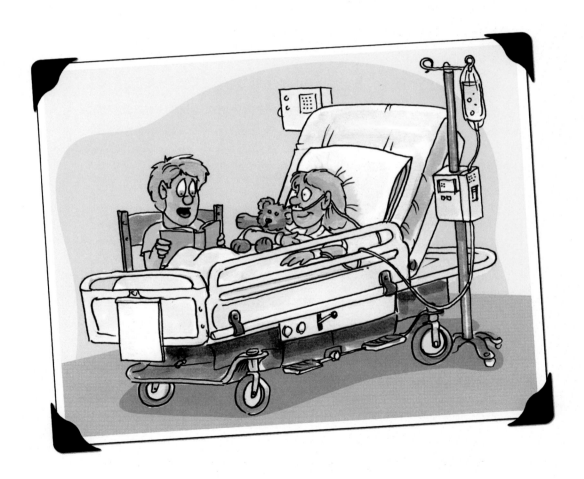

She opened the page to a day full of gloom
when Jamie was sick in a hospital room,
hooked up to machines and enclosed in a mask
as doctors and nurses worked hard at their task.
And outside the room in the midst of despair
sat her sister and brother with heads bowed in prayer.
"Remember the time when you could not get well?
Remember the kindness of Andrew and Michelle?
This photo of you in the hospital bed
shows Andrew with books that he sat down and read.
Michelle shared her dolls and sang you a song.
She gave you some hugs and she said to be strong.
And here is a picture of when you got better.
Your sister and brother wrote such a sweet letter.
So, don't be upset. Let's go make a treat.
I'll finish our dinner and then we can eat."
Small Jamie felt happy and snacked on a pear,
then went to her bedroom to play with her bear.
Her mama, so glad that the problem was fixed,
returned to the kitchen to get the sauce mixed.
She jumped as she heard a loud bang in the hall.
Papa was home and not happy at all.
"Mama, oh Mama, I've had a bad day.

I work all the time and I just want to play.

There's too much to do and I can't get it done.

The phone rings all day, and my job is no fun.

The kids need new shoes, and the roof needs repair.

I think of my youth when I had not a care."

He dropped all his papers and plopped in the chair,

so, Mama again got the scrapbook to share.

"Now see this fun photo of us in the snow?

We played all day long. No one wanted to go.

And here are the kids with your Father's Day card.

They put up a sign over there in the yard.

And look at this picture of you on the floor.

You're all playing games, and you're laughing for more.

So, don't feel so sad. It's just been a bad day.

Go find all the kids and they'll ask you to play."

So, Papa felt better and kissed his kind wife.

He knew he was lucky to have a good life.

They all came together to get the meal ready

with bread sticks, and salad, and lots of spaghetti.

They sat at the table, and shared joy and sorrow,

and planned what to do with another tomorrow.

The scrapbook of photos remained on the shelf,
and Mama looked over and thought to herself,
"It's great to be Mama. I've had a good day.
My family is happy. I like it that way."

HOW TO FEED A HUNGRY GIANT

Tater McCall was a happy man who lived in a tiny cabin near a wide lake in the northern mountains. He was quite content to get up early in the morning, work on his daily chores and then play his fiddle on the porch as the sun disappeared behind the mountains.

Every year, he planted a garden full of green beans, potatoes, tomatoes, peas, carrots, celery, onions, and corn. Green and red apples grew in his orchard, and juicy raspberries hung from bushes around his front door. Tater owned a cow named Bella that produced sweet milk, and two chickens named Clucky and Lucky that laid extra-large eggs.

Tater traveled to a nearby village once a week to trade some of his fruit and vegetables for sacks of flour to make bread. He baked delicious bread. The people loved the smell and taste of his golden-brown loaves, made with wheat, honey, and spices.

In the village, he heard stories about a terrible giant who lived

in the mountains. At the end of each summer, the village people heard loud rumblings and felt the earth tremble. Everyone was afraid to go near the forest because they thought the giant would eat them for dinner.

One autumn morning, Tater was working in his garden when he heard loud noises coming from the mountains. He decided to discover what was causing the horrible sounds. He filled his backpack with a loaf of bread, some apples and vegetables and started on a long hike.

He walked through the trees for several hours and then came to a big hill. After climbing up the hill, he sat down to think. Suddenly, he felt the rumbling right underneath him. Tumbling off the hill, he landed in a pile of leaves. He watched in amazement as the hill moved and a huge giant sat up. Tater had been sitting on top of his belly!

The giant rubbed his stomach, which was rumbling quite loudly.

"Who is there?" growled the giant in a deep voice.

"It is me, Tater." He stood up bravely and waved at the giant.

The giant reached down and scooped up Tater in the palm of his hand. Tater saw that the giant was as big as a house and in need of a bath. The giant's pants and shirt were made from blankets sewn with ropes, and his shoes were hollowed-out logs.

"Why do you make such loud noises?" asked Tater.

"I am hungry," answered the giant. "I need a big meal before I go into my cave to sleep for the winter. You look like a tasty snack." The giant licked his lips.

"Oh, no," replied Tater. "I would not taste good. Here, try my fresh bread."

Tater opened his backpack and took out the wheat loaf. The giant ate it in two bites.

"I like that bread," sighed the giant. "What else do you have?"

Tater gave the giant all his apples and vegetables. The giant was happy for a moment, but then his stomach rumbled again.

"I want more," said the giant, his big eyes squinting at Tater.

"Well, come home with me and I will fix you a wonderful meal. But first, please tell me your name."

"I have no name," mumbled the giant.

"That's not right," exclaimed Tater. "Then I will name you. You should be George. George the Giant."

George the Giant looked pleased. He liked the name. "But I'm still hungry," he said.

"My home is just over those mountains. If we hurry, I'll fix you dinner. Then you will sleep all winter."

The giant tucked Tater in his pocket and stepped over the trees to get to Tater's home.

"Please wash up for dinner," Tater said. "The lake is warm this time of year."

The giant lowered Tater to the ground, then fell into the lake. As he did so, more than 50 fish splashed onto the shore. Tater gathered the fish and began to fix dinner.

After starting a huge fire in a pit in front of his cabin, Tater cleaned the fish, wrapped them in cornhusks from the garden and stuck them in the warm coals. Then he loaded sacks of flour into several washtubs, mixed in the ingredients for bread, and set the tubs in the sunshine. Finally, he brought his bathtub outside, washed it, placed it on the hot coals, and filled it with water.

As the water was heating, he went to his garden and picked all the vegetables he could push in his cart. He dumped potatoes, carrots, celery, onions, tomatoes, peas, corn, and beans into the bathtub. Then he took the bread dough and formed 50 loaves. After placing them on boards over the hot coals, he turned the washtubs upside down to cover the bread so it could bake.

"I'm hungry," called George the Giant as he crawled out of the lake.

"Just be patient," said Tater. "Good food takes time."

"But I'm hungry now," he growled. "Can I eat your cow?"

Bella the cow ran and hid in the apple orchard.

"No, no!" exclaimed Tater. "Then we would have no milk."

"Can I eat your chickens?"

Clucky and Lucky scrambled under the porch, squawking wildly.

"No, no! Then we would have no eggs."

A big tear rolled down the giant's cheek, splashed on the ground and almost put out the fire.

"Wait just a minute," called Tater as he went into his cabin.

He returned with his fiddle, sat on a stump, and began to play. George sat down in the meadow beside the cabin. As the air filled with happy tunes and the smell of baking bread, the giant smiled.

Finally, it was time to eat. Tater spread several blankets over the ground, placed log planks on top of them and set out the food. The giant ate the 50 fish, gobbled down the 50 loaves of bread, and drank all the vegetable soup from the bathtub. He finished his meal with five gallons of milk and several jugs of apple juice, then he patted his stomach, stretched out in the meadow and took a long nap.

It was almost evening when the giant awoke. Tater had cleaned up all the mess from the meal and was playing his fiddle on the porch of his cabin.

"Thank you for the good meal," said the giant. "I will sleep all winter long and not be hungry."

Tater was happy that the giant enjoyed his dinner.

"I hope you are full because there is no more food," said Tater. "But my garden will grow more. Please come back again."

Then George leaned over and pulled out some trees. He broke off the limbs and piled the logs near Tater's small cabin.

"Make yourself a bigger cabin," said the giant. "And plant some trees to replace these."

Then the giant dragged his hand through the land where the trees had been growing. He plowed rows in the dirt with his fingers.

"Make yourself a bigger garden," he said. "And plant it in the spring."

Then George the Giant waved his big hand and walked back toward the mountains. The cow and the chickens came out from their hiding places.

The next day, Tater started to build his new cabin with the giant's logs. The cabin was finished when the first snows of winter began to fall. Tater was cozy and dry, and his pantry was full of fruits and vegetables.

In the spring, Tater planted more crops in his big garden and worked hard all summer. By autumn, he had plenty of food.

One day, he heard familiar rumbling from the mountains. He prepared the fire and began to fix the giant's meal. When he saw the giant stepping over the trees, Tater waved. He noticed the giant was carrying a large sack.

"Here is a gift for you," George said with a grin. He unwrapped the sack and out jumped some goats, two cows, a horse, and a few pigs. "I found these lost in the mountains," he explained, shrugging his shoulders. "You can have them."

The giant pulled out more trees and created fences to hold the animals. Then he jumped in the lake to wash for dinner. After his bath, the giant sat down to his favorite meal: bread, fish, and vegetable soup. As usual, he took a long nap then happily walked back to his cave.

Tater lived well for many years. Every fall, he would prepare a meal for the giant. In return, George would bring him animals or build fences or clear land. Tater soon had the biggest ranch in the valley.

The village people came from miles around to hear about the giant and to sample delicious, homemade bread. Tater would sit on his porch, play his fiddle, and tell stories until the moon was high in the sky. It was a good life, and he was happy.

BIKING TO THE MOON

Emily couldn't sleep. The full moon made her bedroom almost as bright as day, and she wasn't tired at all. She closed her eyes and tried to remember how sleepy she became after swimming all day at the YMCA. That didn't work.

So, she imagined she was floating on a cloud listening to the boring music she had heard at the dentist's office while waiting with her mother. Still, she was wide-awake.

She hugged Buttons the Bear for comfort, but the toy, too, seemed ready to play. The fluffy, white bear was her favorite present from her eighth birthday party just two weeks earlier. The bear wore a red vest with brass buttons and fit perfectly in the basket on her red bicycle. On these sunny summer days, they traveled all around the neighborhood and the nearby park. They also liked to hide under the big lilac tree in the backyard.

The bear was her best friend because she didn't have any sisters, only three brothers. There weren't any girls in the neighborhood to play with during the summer. Sometimes Emily talked with Buttons. And the stuffed toy talked back to her.

Emily still couldn't sleep. She crawled out of bed and sat in the window seat. Tucking her pink nightgown around her knees, she brushed back her long blonde hair and stared out the window. Buttons stared, too.

The moonlight made strange shadows in the lawn. Then she saw something shine in the light. It was her bike. She gasped because she had left it outside. It was her responsibility to put it in the garage every night. She knew her parents would be upset with her if they saw the bike outside in the morning. There was only one thing to do.

Emily quietly turned on the little light next to her bed and changed into jeans, a sweatshirt, and tennis shoes. Grabbing Buttons, she tiptoed down the hall. She stopped at her parents' bedroom door but there was no sound. She moved slowly past her brothers' bedrooms then tiptoed down the stairs. The moonlight gave her just enough light to see into the kitchen. Hugging Buttons, she crossed the floor and opened the door into the garage.

The garage looked like a big black hole and she hesitated. Maybe she should go back to bed and not worry about the bicycle.

Buttons clapped her paws. "Just say it four times again. It's easy!"

Emily looked around. No one was outside to stop her. She pushed Buttons down in the basket, firmly grabbed the handlebars, and whispered,

"Sing a tune about the moon,
Seize the day and fly away!"

"Sing a tune about the moon,
Seize the day and fly away!"

Suddenly the bike started to move. The wheels turned around and then the bike lifted into the air. Emily squealed in delight and watched as the houses passed beneath her. The bike soared over the park and she could see the swings in the moonlight. Then the bike went faster and flew straight up toward the moon.

"Yippee!" yelled Emily as the bike got closer to the bright moon. As they came near land, she could see a big door hidden on the side of a round crater. The door opened and the bike disappeared inside. Emily found herself in a large room full of old people.

"Who are you?" asked Emily, a bit breathless from her trip. Buttons peeked over the basket rim and waved to the crowd.

An old man moved slowly over to Emily.

"We've been waiting for you, Emily," he said. He smiled at the girl and patted Buttons on the head. "We are old and lonely and we were waiting for a child to come and visit us."

Then an old woman approached with a tray of cookies. "I made these for you," she said. "They're only 200 years old, and they're still good. Would you like some milk?"

"No, thank you," Emily said. "I've already brushed my teeth."

Then another woman approached. "Will you read to me?" she asked, handing her a tattered book.

"No, it's my turn," said a plump old man with a shy grin. "Please sing to me. Any song will do."

Then others came forward with similar requests.

"Can we ride your bike?"

"Play ball with us."

"Can you tell us a story?"

Emily was confused with all the requests and she didn't know what to do.

Just then a tall woman clapped her hands and the group stepped back. "Please forgive us, Emily," said the woman. "We have been waiting for a child to play with us. We're so happy you are here."

"Who are you?" whispered Emily. She stared at the woman who was dressed in a shimmering purple gown that trailed onto the floor. The woman's face glowed with warmth and her white hair flowed down her back. She wore a crown of fresh lilacs.

"I am Queen Lilah. We were sent here centuries ago by an evil curse from a nasty troll named Terrible Tom. Our fate was to wait for you to come." She smiled and touched Emily on the cheek.

"I have to go home soon," Emily explained. "But I can play for a while."

Emily talked with the people, read to them, sang songs, and laughed at their jokes. She listened to their stories and allowed them to hold Buttons the Bear. They all had a wonderful time.

Then Queen Lilah stood up and raised her hand. "It's time for you to go now," she said. "The moon is fading." The queen touched Emily's hair and placed some lilac flowers behind her ear.

With that, the group waved at Emily and clapped their hands. They smiled, blew kisses and called out "Thank you for breaking the spell." Emily poked Buttons down in the basket and grabbed the handlebars. She repeated four times:

"Sing a tune about the moon,
Seize the day and fly away!"

"Sing a tune about the moon,
Seize the day and fly away!"

"Sing a tune about the moon,
Seize the day and fly away!"

"Sing a tune about the moon,
Seize the day and fly away!"

Suddenly the bike moved and the door opened. Emily went flying into space and down toward earth. After a few circles around the park, the bike landed softly on her driveway. She looked up at the moon in amazement, and then hurried into the garage. After securing her bike, she tiptoed inside the house and moved quietly to her room. She wiggled out of her clothes and into her nightgown. She hugged Buttons and fell fast asleep.

Mrs. Malone, the babysitter, came to the house every day in the summer while Emily's parents were at work. The day after Emily's adventure, the woman marched up to Emily's bedroom. "Wake up, Emily," she called as she entered the room. "You've slept the entire morning, and it's almost time for lunch."

Emily rubbed her eyes and sat up in bed. Mrs. Malone was standing with her hands on her hips. "Do you feel okay child?" the woman asked.

"Oh, yes, Mrs. Malone. I just had the strangest dream!" She hopped from the bed and ran to the window. Her bicycle was not in the yard. "I dreamed that I rode my bike to the moon!"

"Such silliness!" exclaimed the woman. "Now get dressed and come and eat. It's a beautiful summer day and you should be playing outside."

After eating, Emily grabbed Buttons and rode her bike to the park. As she played on the swings, she thought about old people, Queen Lilah, and flying through space to the moon. Was it just a dream?

She rode her bicycle back home just as her mother was driving into the garage. "It looks like we have new neighbors," her mother said. A moving van was backed up to the home next door.

Emily watched as two men moved furniture into the house. Then a girl came out of the door and waved at Emily. She walked across the lawn, carrying a stuffed, yellow bunny with long, floppy ears. The girl's bouncy brown ponytail was tied with a purple ribbon.

"Hi," she said. "My name is Lilah. I'm eight years old. Who are you?"

"I'm Emily. And I'm eight years old, too!"

"Do you want to ride bikes?" asked Lilah.

"Sure! I'll show you around," offered Emily. She already liked her new neighbor.

Emily and Lilah spent the rest of the summer riding bikes, playing in the park, and having secret meetings under the lilac bush. With the stuffed bear and the floppy rabbit, they had fun adventures until dark. By autumn, they were the best of friends.

One night, the harvest moon poured into Emily's bedroom window. She awoke from another strange dream. "Just go back to sleep," whispered Buttons the Bear. "It was only a dream."

As Emily reached over to hug her bear, she noticed something in the moonlight. A sprig of fresh lilacs rested on her pillow.

GATORS & TATERS - CREATED TO BE READ ALOUD TO A CHILD

Celebrate the tradition of storytelling and inspire children to wonder about characters, places, and adventures. These seven delightful stories bubble with lyrical language, captivating scenes, and gentle messages. No batteries required.

AWARDS AND HONORS FOR GATORS & TATERS

One of 50 Children's Books Selected for Bowker's National Recommended Reading List

Selected for Idaho Public Television "First Books" Program with Statewide distribution to underprivileged children

Selected for State of Idaho "Read Out Loud Crowd" Program

Selected for the Summer Reading List for the Log Cabin Literary Center in Boise, Idaho

Selected for the Barnes & Noble Summer Reading Program in Boise, Idaho

ABOUT THE AUTHOR

Elaine Ambrose is a #1 bestselling author of eight books, including *The Magic Potato – La Papa Mágica,* a bilingual storybook adopted for the Idaho statewide school curriculum. A visit to Ireland sparked her interest in folklore and inspired *Gators & Taters,* a collection of stories she told to her children and now reads to her grandchildren. Elaine lives and eats potatoes in Idaho.

EBook and Audiobook are also available.

HERE ARE SOME DISCUSSION SUBJECTS FOR PARENTS, CAREGIVERS, AND TEACHERS TO SHARE WITH CHILDREN AFTER READING THE STORIES ALOUD.

GATORS & TATERS

Can you imagine two alligators playing in a potato field?

Have you ever been to a farm?

Do you think Wendell O'Doodle became happy again
on the Oregon Coast?

Describe a traveling adventure you have enjoyed.

THE BIRTHDAY BOY

Do you have a favorite birthday memory or present?

Can you imagine how this boy felt as he grew older?
What age do you want to be?

How do you celebrate birthdays in your family?

Describe how each family member reacted to the boy's birthday.

HOOTENFLOOT FLIES THE COOP

Would you like to meet Miss Bitterpenny and Miss Wobblefloss? Why?

Why did Hootenfloot fly away?

Can you imagine eating sausage strudel or a bramble plum?

Describe why Hootenfloot was so sad after he ran away, and then why everyone was so happy when they all got back together.

THE SECRET READING ROOM

Have you ever worked on a project with a grandparent or other family member? Can you imagine canning food for the pantry?

Would you like to have a secret reading room? How would you decorate it?

What places do you want to visit? Why?

Describe how you would get to know children from other countries.

MAMA, I've HAD A BAD DAY!

Have you ever had a bad day? What happened?
How did you get happy again?

What happens when your family members or friends have a bad day?

Do you enjoy looking at family photos?

Describe how you feel when you're frustrated and want someone
to listen to you.

HOW TO FEED A HUNGRY GIANT

Can you imagine the life of Tater McCall?
Have you ever played an instrument or planted a garden?

What would you do if you saw a giant?

Could you eat 50 loaves of bread?

Explain how Tater McCall entertained the giant
and the people of the village.

BIKING TO THE MOON

Have you ever had trouble going to sleep?

Can you imagine riding your bike up to the moon?

Have you ever made new friends?

Describe how Emily felt as she rode through the air
with her talking bear.